CARTWRIGHT CENTRAL P.S
LIBRARY

Backyard Animals
Wolves

Edited by Heather C. Hudak

Weigl Publishers Inc.

Published by Weigl Publishers Inc.
350 5th Avenue, Suite 3304, PMB 6G
New York, NY 10118-0069
Website: www.weigl.com

Copyright ©2009 WEIGL PUBLISHERS INC.
All rights reserved. No part of this publication may be reproduced, stored in a retrieval system, or transmitted in any form or by any means, electronic, mechanical, photocopying, recording, or otherwise, without the prior written permission of the publisher.

Library of Congress Cataloging-in-Publication Data available upon request.
Fax 1-866-44-WEIGL for the attention of the Publishing Records department.

ISBN 978-1-60596-005-0 (hard cover)
ISBN 978-1-60596-011-1 (soft cover)

Printed in the United States of America
1 2 3 4 5 6 7 8 9 0   12 11 10 09 08

Editor Heather C. Hudak
Design Terry Paulhus

All of the Internet URLs given in the book were valid at the time of publication. However, due to the dynamic nature of the Internet, some addresses may have changed, or sites may have ceased to exist since publication. While the author and publisher regret any inconvenience this may cause readers, no responsibility for any such changes can be accepted by either the author or the publisher.

Photo Credits

Weigl acknowledges Getty Images as its primary image supplier for this title.

Every reasonable effort has been made to trace ownership and to obtain permission to reprint copyright material. The publishers would be pleased to have any errors or omissions brought to their attention so that they may be corrected in subsequent printings.

Contents

Meet the Wolf 4

All about Wolves 6

Wolf History 8

Wolf Habitat 10

Wolf Features 12

What Do Wolves Eat? 14

Wolf Life Cycle 16

Encountering Wolves 18

Myths and Legends 20

Frequently Asked Questions 22

Puzzler/Find Out More 23

Words to Know/Index 24

Meet the Wolf

Wolves are **mammals**. They are large doglike animals that move around in **packs**. They are powerful hunters and fast runners.

Wolves have long snouts and pointed ears. Their sense of smell and hearing is very good. They use these senses to find food. Wolves usually live in colder parts of the world. They have thick, coarse fur that helps keep them warm.

Wolves are known for their loud, long howl. They use their howl to **communicate** with each other. A lone wolf howls to get in touch with its pack. A pack of wolves howls together to communicate with other packs.

Wolves have different types of howls. Each has its own meaning.

There are often eight or nine wolves in a pack. However, packs with 20 to 30 wolves have been found.

All about Wolves

The wolf is from the same family as the dog. They are both **canines**. There are different **species** of wolf all over the world. Wolves can be found in China, Russia, northern Europe, Canada, and the United States. Some species of wolf are very rare. They can only be found in certain parts of the world. The Abyssinian wolf only lives in the mountain regions of Ethiopia in Africa.

Gray wolves and red wolves live in the United States. The gray wolf is more common than the red wolf. There are many types of gray wolf, including the Arctic wolf and the Mexican wolf.

Gray wolves are the most common type of wolf in the world.

Where Wolves Live

Arctic Wolf
- Found in the snowy regions of northern Canada and Greenland

Gray Wolf
- Lives in the forests of North America, Europe, Asia, and the Middle East

Red Wolf
- Lives in the southeastern United States, from Texas to Florida

Mexican Wolf
- Found in the mountainous forests and woodlands of the southwestern United States

Wolf History

The earliest canines lived around 60 million years ago. One of the first canines was the dawn-wolf. The dawn-wolf looked like a fox and could climb trees.

There are many canine species that have become **extinct** over time. Changes in the weather made it difficult for these animals to survive, and some of the early species died.

Scientists are still trying to find out where wolves first lived. Many think that the first gray wolf traveled from Asia or Europe to North America about 7,000 years ago.

The Himalayan wolf is the world's oldest species of wolf. Scientists believe that it first appeared about 800,000 years ago.

Wolves have thick fur that helps protect them from harsh weather. Snow slides off without melting into the wolf's fur.

Wolf Habitat

Wolves mostly live in cold climates, where there are few people. Some wolves live in warmer climates, such as Mexico, Greece, or India.

Wolves live in dens. Dens can be made in between large rocks, inside a hollow log, or under the overhang of a cliff. Wolves can use the same den for many years.

The area that a wolf lives in is called its **territory**. This territory can be up to 70 square miles (112 square kilometers). Wolves have many rules about how each pack controls its own territory. They will fight wolves and other animals to maintain their space.

Wolves have **adapted** to live any place they can find **prey**. However, they prefer to live where there are plenty of bushes and trees.

Arctic wolves have white fur, which helps them blend into their snowy surroundings.

Wolves like to live near water and places where they can find prey easily.

Wolf Features

Wolves are some of the best **predators** in the animal kingdom. This is because they have many features that help them run fast, find prey, and survive in nature.

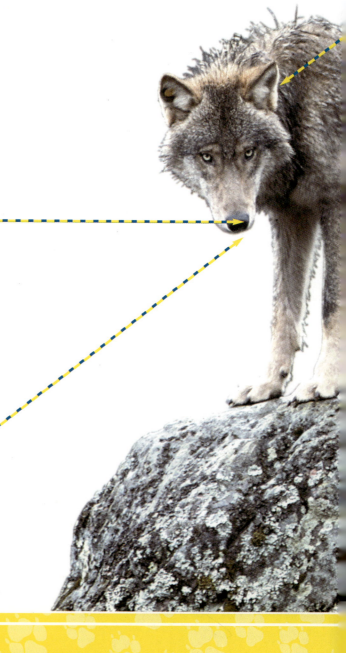

NOSE
Wolves have a strong sense of smell. They use it as a tool to find food. They can smell animals that are more than 1 mile (1.6 km) away.

MOUTH
Wolves have very sharp teeth to help them tear meat from their prey. This also makes it easy for them to carry prey long distances to the rest of the pack.

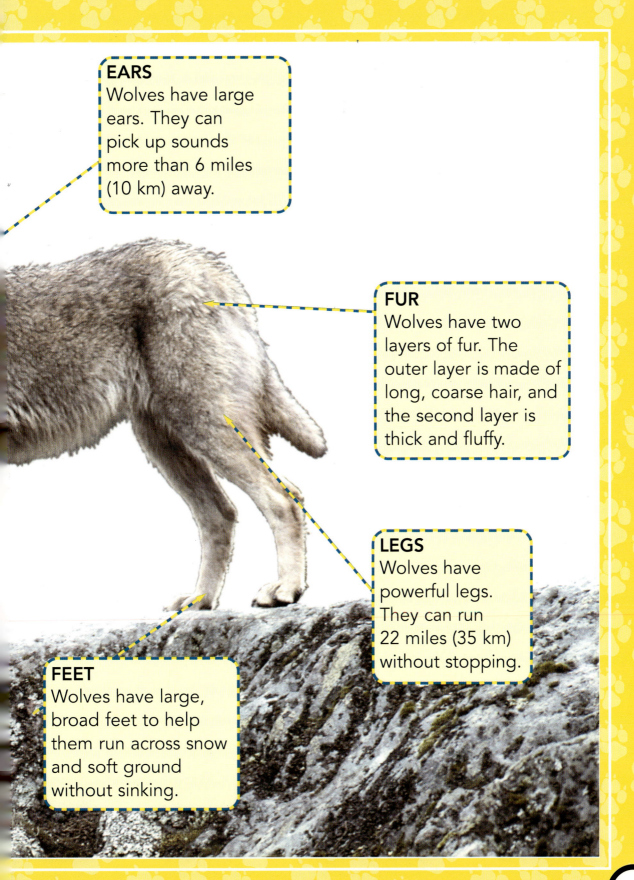

EARS
Wolves have large ears. They can pick up sounds more than 6 miles (10 km) away.

FUR
Wolves have two layers of fur. The outer layer is made of long, coarse hair, and the second layer is thick and fluffy.

LEGS
Wolves have powerful legs. They can run 22 miles (35 km) without stopping.

FEET
Wolves have large, broad feet to help them run across snow and soft ground without sinking.

What Do Wolves Eat?

Wolves are carnivores. This means that their diet is made up mainly of meat.

Depending on the place where they live, wolves hunt different types of prey. Often, the prey that they hunt is much bigger than the wolves. To help with this, wolves hunt in packs. This lets them take down larger animals. Wolves also make sure to hunt weaker targets. Small or sick animals are easier to catch.

A wolf can eat almost 20 percent of its body weight in one meal.

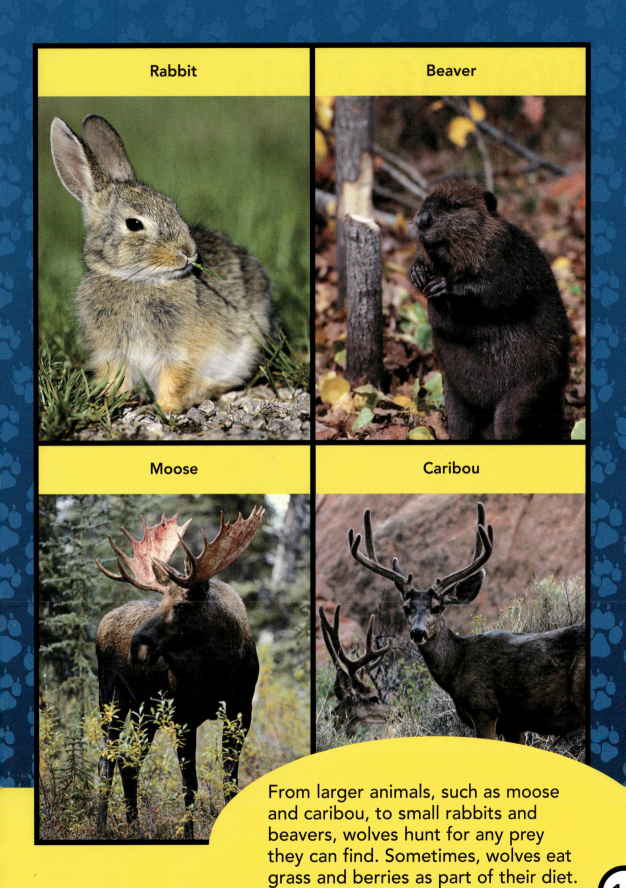

From larger animals, such as moose and caribou, to small rabbits and beavers, wolves hunt for any prey they can find. Sometimes, wolves eat grass and berries as part of their diet.

Wolf Life Cycle

Wolves live for about 7 to 10 years. Once a wolf reaches two years old, it can start to mate. However, only the strongest male and female in a pack will breed. They are known as the alpha male and the alpha female.

Birth

The female digs a den where she will give birth to her pups. She can give birth to between 3 and 14 pups in one litter. Wolf pups spend their first two months sleeping and feeding on their mother's milk. They can barely open their eyes, and their sense of smell is weak.

Transition

After two weeks, the pups begin to open their eyes. They eat meat that the adults carry back to the den in their stomachs. The adults **regurgitate** the food for the pups. At this time, the pups learn to stand and howl.

The males in the pack fight each other to find out who is the strongest. The most powerful male becomes the alpha male.

Socialization

The pups slowly meet the rest of the pack. They begin play-fighting with other pups. Their fur starts to grow, and they are able to eat the same meat as the adults.

Juvenile period

By nine months, the pups have their full fur and start to hunt for their own meat. Their teeth begin to get sharper, and the pups are almost the same size as the adults. The pups are considered adults when they are about two years old.

Encountering Wolves

People may see wolves when they are exploring in nature. At times, people may even come across an entire pack of wolves.

Wolves do not often live in places where there are many humans. Unlike other animals, wolves do not run away when they see humans. Instead, they become alert and may even attack if they sense any danger. If you see a wolf, it is best to keep your distance and try to walk to a safe place. Make loud noises to scare the animal away.

Check out this site for more interesting information about wolves.
www.boomerwolf.com

There are very few red wolves living in nature. They are in danger of becoming extinct.

Myths and Legends

There are plenty of stories in which wolves are seen as dangerous and wicked. Many children's stories and fairy tales have a mean wolf character. In these stories, wolves are greedy and evil animals. The wolf in the story of *Little Red Riding Hood* tries to eat the girl and her grandmother.

However, some stories also show how wolves can be good examples. The mother wolf in *The Jungle Book* looks after Mowgli, the human child, along with her cubs.

Red Riding Hood meets the Big Bad Wolf while walking through the woods.

The Myth of Romulus and Remus

Romulus and Remus were twin brothers. As babies, their parents put them in a basket on the Tiber River. The basket slowly drifted onto the riverbank, where the twins were discovered by a female wolf. The wolf cared for the babies until a shepherd found them. The shepherd raised the twins.

When Romulus and Remus grew up, they decided to build a city where the wolf had found them. Once they built the city, the brothers argued about what it should be called. They both wanted to name it after themselves. In the end, Romulus won the fight. He became the king of the new city and named it "Rome" in his honor. This is how the city of Rome was founded.

Frequently Asked Questions

How big are wolves?

Answer: An adult male wolf can range in size from 80 to 110 pounds (36 to 40 kilograms). Female wolves are slightly smaller. Size varies depending on the type of wolf.

Can I keep a wolf as a pet?

Answer: Wolves are not meant to be kept as pets. They may look similar to dogs, but wolves are used to living in nature and have not been **domesticated**. Most wolves are too afraid of people to be kept as pets.

Why are wolves becoming endangered?

Answer: Wolves are becoming **endangered** for many reasons. People are building cities on the land where wolves live. This forces them away from their territories. Wolves are not able to find prey, and they starve. People also hunt wolves.

Puzzler

See if you can answer these questions about wolves.

1. What type of animal is a wolf?
2. What is the most common species of wolf?
3. Which household pet is the wolf most like?
4. How many wolves are in a pack?
5. What is special about a wolf's coat?

Answers: 1. mammal 2. gray wolf 3. the dog 4. usually eight or nine but as many as 30 5. It has two layers, one coarse outside layer, and one thick layer underneath.

Find Out More

There are many more interesting facts to learn about wolves. Look for these books at your library so you can find out more.

Evert, Laura, and John F. McGee. *Wolves*. T & N Children's Publishing, 2000.

Simon, Seymour. *Wolves*. Harper Collins Publishers, 1995.

Words to Know

adapted: adjusted to the natural environment
canines: a family of mammals that include the dog and the fox
communicate: to make sounds in order to share information
domesticated: trained to live with people
endangered: to be at risk of disappearing
extinct: no longer living on Earth
mammals: warm-blooded animals that have a backbone and drink milk from their mother
packs: groups of wolves
predators: animals that hunt other animals
prey: an animal that is hunted for food
regurgitate: when food is eaten, stored in the stomach, and then spit out
species: a group of animals or plants that have many features in common
territory: the land on which a pack of wolves lives and hunts

Index

canines 6, 8

dens 10, 16

fur 4, 8, 10, 13, 17

gray wolf 6, 7, 8, 23

howl 4, 16

packs 4, 5, 10, 12, 14, 16, 17, 18, 23

prey 10, 11, 12, 14, 15, 22

pups 16, 17

red wolf 6, 7, 19